DANNY DIAMONDBACK

by Barry E. Jackson

HarperCollins *Publishers*

Way out yonder, in the harsh, cruel desert, there lived a little rattlesnake named Danny Diamondback. One day his ma and pa decided to go to a nearby town to coil up behind the drive-in picture show.

They kissed Danny on the nose and slithered off. Sadly, when Danny awoke the next morning, his parents were nowhere to be found.

At sundown a crow landed on a tree near Danny's home.

"Your mammy and pappy got caught by human folk and are livin' at the zoo! They say you got to go out and make a life for yourself now."

Terrified, Danny wedged his head into a corner and shut his eyes. But after a while, he reckoned his ma and pa knew best. So for the first time, he slid out of the rock nest and entered the wide world.

Danny went no farther than a stone's throw before he spied a couple of jackrabbits.

Rattlin' his tail, Danny hissed, "Excuse me, y'all. . . . I was wondering if maybe you'd like to be my new ma and pa?"

Them jackrabbits tore a hole through the sagebrush faster than a bolt of lightnin'!

Puzzled, Danny shook his head. You see, his ma and pa had never told him he was a deadly poisonous snake.

Later Danny spotted a family of sparrows. Coilin' round the tree trunk, he worked his way upward and peered all shy-like from behind a branch.

Danny rattled his tail. "Hey, y'all," he hissed. "How 'bout a game of Twister?"

Them birds screeched in horror and shot like bullets in all directions. Danny wondered if he had forgotten to brush his teeth.

For days every critter Danny met ran from him in terror. Danny slid sadly on until he spied a town of prairie dogs.

"Pardon me," Danny hissed, rattlin' his tail. "Y'all have the loveliest neighborhood. Would you prairie dogs perchance mind a guest?"

When the dust settled, Danny looked around to find himself alone again. Hearin' a voice, he looked over to see a prairie dog sifting through the sand with his paws.

The little prairie dog cried, "Help! Help! I can't find my glasses!"

Danny slithered over. "Where'd you last see 'em?"

Without his glasses, the prairie dog thought Danny was a lizard. "My name is Pablo," he said. "You must be new to these parts."

Danny introduced himself but declined to shake hands, sayin' he had a cold.

Pablo invited Danny to his house.

"I got me another pair of glasses . . . ," murmured
Pablo. He felt around and placed his hand on a trumpet.
"Can you play it?" asked Danny.
Pablo played a little tune.
Downright dazzled, Danny wanted to clap, but
since he couldn't, he unfortunately did something else.
He rattled his tail.

A big grandma prairie dog burst in and commenced to shriekin'
like her tail was afire! Then a big ol' bullfrog landed between Pablo
and Danny, throwin' roundhouse kicks!

"No!" cried Pablo. "He is my amigo!"

The hullabaloo simmered.

"Okay, Pablo," sighed the old grandma. "He can stay for one
day . . . but our neighbors better not learn that you've made
friends with a rattlesnake!"

The next day Danny tried not to rattle his tail. He tried to be helpful-like. He straightened up Pablo's room, swept the floor, and helped prepare supper. He ate sunflower seeds just like a prairie dog, although at home his ma had served him small bugs.

After supper Pablo's family played music. Danny wanted to play too, so Pablo tried him out on the piccolo. Danny didn't do so well, not havin' any fingers and all.

"*Amigo*," said the bullfrog. "I think you can play those rattles on your tail."

"You mean these?" asked Danny.

"*Si. Maracas!*" said the bullfrog with a laugh. Then he got out a pair of bongo drums and showed Danny some Latin rhythm. Although at first a mite wayward, Danny learned how to rattle at just the right moment.

Danny gave a new spark to their music!

"*Amigos!*" bellowed the bullfrog. "Let's take this new music on the road!"

"With a rattlesnake?" gasped the grandma.

The bullfrog slapped a big sombrero on Danny's head and laughed. "With this on, who's going to know?"

They called themselves the Hoppin' Jalapeños.
The next night they played a small rock crevice.

The next thing you know, bugs commenced to flyin' far and wide, spreading the news. For a spell, the critters in those parts laid down their hostile ways and took to dancin'.

Danny finally fit in—that is, until he forgot he was a rattlesnake. One night, lost in the rhythm, he flung his head back and sent his sombrero a-flyin'. He gyrated in front of all those critters, fangs a-gleamin' and tail a-rattlin'.

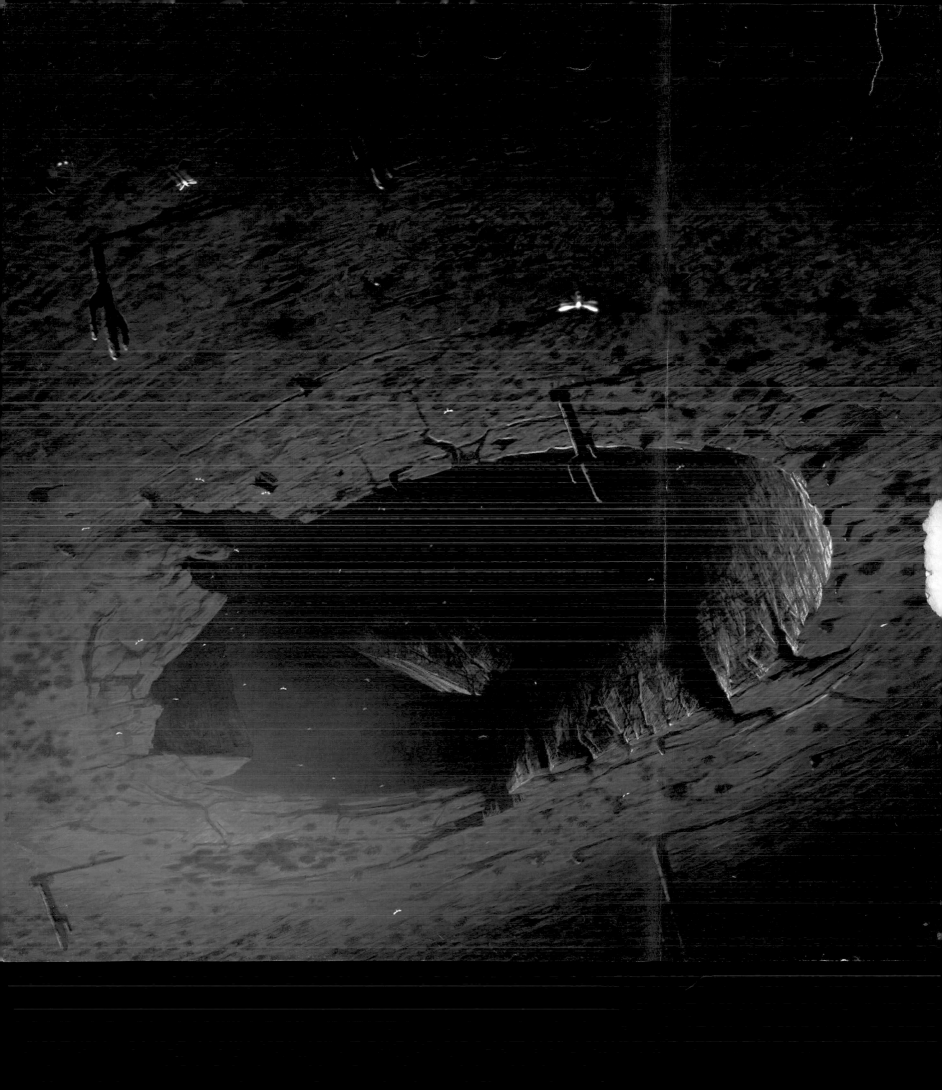

"He'll kill us all!" squealed the kangaroo rat.

Sunrise found Danny alone again. The peculiar ways of other critters finally had him beat. He reckoned he'd head for the hills alone. Turnin' away, he caught a glimpse of a desert tortoise.

"Oh, Mr. Tortoise?" called Danny. "Why don't folks like rattlesnakes?"

"Well, sonny," replied the tortoise slowly, "they strike quicker than lightnin.' Their bite can kill a horse, and if that ain't enough, they are the only critter bold enough to warn you before they kill you!"

Danny gasped. "Is that what them rattles is for?"

The tortoise laughed. "Of course! Even a gadfly knows that!"

Three months later, feelin' lower than a snake's belly, Danny lay under a rock up in the hills. He tried to remember the good times.

Suddenly coyote howls pierced the sky. Over yonder, Danny spied a whole pack of them sniffin' low to the ground and headed in the direction of Pablo's home.

Danny remembered his friends and high-tailed it for the prairie dog town.

Them coyotes swaggered into town, hungry for a picnic.
Out popped Danny, hissin' and a-rattlin' like no tomorrow!
The coyotes leaped back. Then they sized up this ornery
critter. They noticed the rhythm of Danny's rattlin'.
"You ain't that maraca player from the Hoppin' Jalapeños,
are ya?" asked the leader.
"Dad gum if I ain't!" said Danny.

"Well, whup me with a hickory stick!" cried the leader. "Any chance we can get an autograph?"

"If you leave the prairie dogs be," answered Danny.

"Not a problem!" cried them coyotes. Danny signed autographs for the whole pack. The coyotes moseyed on, happy to have met a famous musician.

The prairie dogs rose to stand in awe of their new hero,
Danny Diamondback. The mayor called for a fiesta.

And don't you know, that fiesta was more fun than a hog-callin' contest in Tuscaloosa! By the end of the night, all them critters was dancin' round in a conga line!

Danny lived the rest of his days with his new friends as musician, protector, and member of the family.

To Rachel Ann Jackson
—B.E.J.

Danny Diamondback

Copyright © 2008 by Barry E. Jackson

Manufactured in China.

All rights reserved. No part of this book may be used or reproduced in any manner

whatsoever without written permission except in the case of brief quotations

embodied in critical articles and reviews. For information address

HarperCollins Children's Books, a division of HarperCollins Publishers,

1350 Avenue of the Americas, New York, NY 10019.

www.harpercollinschildrens.com

Library of Congress Cataloging—in—Publication Data is available.

ISBN-10: 0-06-113184-9 (trade bdg.) — ISBN-13: 978-0-06-113184-4 (trade bdg.)

ISBN-10: 0-06-113185-7 (lib. bdg.) — ISBN-13: 978-0-06-113185-1 (lib. bdg.)

Typography by Amelia May Anderson

1 2 3 4 5 6 7 8 9 10   ❖   First Edition